Skit Skit Skitterarich

illustrated by
Denis Proulx

written by
Crystal Keogan

Wasteland Press
www.wastelandpress.net
Shelbyville, KY USA

Skit Skit Skitterarich
by Crystal Keogan

Copyright © 2015 Crystal Keogan
ALL RIGHTS RESERVED

First Printing – June 2015
ISBN: 978-1-68111-030-1
Library of Congress Control Number: 2015938564
Cover and interior images by Denis Proulx
www. www.shangrila-studio.com

NO PART OF THIS BOOK MAY BE REPRODUCED IN ANY FORM, BY
PHOTOCOPYING OR BY ANY ELECTRONIC OR MECHANICAL MEANS,
INCLUDING INFORMATION STORAGE OR RETRIEVAL SYSTEMS, WITHOUT
PERMISSION IN WRITING FROM THE COPYRIGHT OWNER/AUTHOR

Printed in the U.S.A.

0 1 2 3 4 5 6

With love to my grandchildren,
who are beautiful, bewildering,
bewitching, and best of all mine...

There once was a boy who lived in the city
in a house surrounded by trees.
He loved to watch chipmunks and squirrels
scamper with the birds and bees.

He could sit and smile every day,
amusing himself by the hour,
watching each little critter bounding along,
or flying from flower to flower.

But one night while alone,
he quit reading to hear
a sound, an ominous tone.
The noise made goose bumps appear.

Skitterarich, skit skit,
skitter skit, skitterarich
skitterarich skitterarich itch.

Could it be dinosaur toenails, mouse whiskers,
a troll's mustache, or the heels of a witch?

Where was it coming from?

Not the halls or the walls;
not his phone, nor his electronic toys.
He wandered around to look and to listen,
until there it was—the very same noise.

Skitterarich skit skit
skitter skit, skitterarich
skitterarich skitterarich itch.

It came from above, over his head,
in the dark and scary attic.

He opened the door and pulled the stairs
to the floor with a puzzling frown.
He climbed up and peeked into the dark,
quite ready to fly back down.
His vision was poor, the cobwebs were thick, and
there was an odd smell in the air,
musty and old, kind of making him sick.
His heart was pounding, he felt such a scare.

He couldn't see—it was dark as pitch,
but then on a gasp, he heard:

Skitterarich skit skit,
skitter skit, skitterarich
skitterarich skitterarich itch.

He saw something move.

He saw something twitch.

Was it dinosaur, a troll,

a mouse, or a witch?

Skitterarich, skit skit
skitter skit, skitterarich
Skitterarich skitterarich itch.

Banging his head and slamming his thumb,
down the ladder he fled,
back the way he had come.

What would Dad do hearing a noise in the night?
Let me think—what to do?
I know—get a light!
He ran to the hall, got a flashlight from there, ran back
to the ladder, and climbed up the stair. His hand was
shaking, but he peeked inside.
The light swirled around, and his eyes opened wide.
There in the corner it skittered and crept.
Then into the light, the fearful thing leapt!

Skitterarich, skit skit
skitter skit, skitterarich
Skitterarich skitterarich itch.

But it was a squirrel—not a dinosaur,
a troll, nor a mouse. Not even a witch.
It was fuzzy and red, a strange little tyke,
with white on his head, and his fur seemed to spike.
He had nails curved and long; now it all seemed to fit.
Mikey was sure he wasn't wrong—he had solved skitter-it.

He must have come through an old venting flap,
but not gone out again, as it closed like a trap.

Mikey slammed down the hatch and jumped to the floor.
His heart was still pounding,
but he now knew what for.

Not a witch that was green, not a dinosaur from history,
not a troll who was mean, nor was a mouse the mystery.

Now he wasn't so scared, as he was worried about how to
help and to spare this guy red and furry.

The squirrel was up there,
so afraid and alone.

The boy knew he wouldn't come down,
oh no, of course, not on his own.

How could he get him to leave?
Take a hike?
What in the world would a small squirrel like?

Was it broccoli?
Or spinach?

Was it cabbage? Or carrots?

Was it chocolate?
Or cupcakes?

I know!
It's NUTS!

He looked in the cupboards,
inside jars and behind tissues.

Not a nut to be found, none were around,
til at last in the fridge he found cashews.
He opened a window and lowered
the ladder to the attic door.

He made a path across the hall
to the window on the floor.
He laid out the cashews
in a long, nutty string.
"Let's see," said the boy,
"what results this will bring."

Then he carefully hid
behind a door to the room,
hoping the squirrel he bid would come down
real soon.
He waited and waited and tried not to sleep.
Finally, he heard a noise and decided to peep.
The sound he now knew
didn't even make him twitch;
That—

Skitterarich skit skit,
skitter skit, skitterarich
skitterarich skitterarich itch.

The squirrel had come down
to the smell of the food,
and he knew he must eat
or that would be rude.

The squirrel was eating and seemed to be happy,
but now the boy had to find
how to set the squirrel free.

"Humm", said the boy.
"I must get him outside,"
and he jumped to his feet.
The squirrel jumped, too,
and stopped moving and couldn't eat.

Waving his hands and shuffling his feet,
the boy tried to get the squirrel to shoo.
But he didn't want the squirrel
to come running by him—would you?

Though small and not a big scare,
the question does beg—
would you want him in your hair
if he ran up your leg?

But the squirrel was scared,
his tail curled high. He kept looking the boy
straight in the eye. The boy stomped his foot
and the fur really flew. Neither knew just
what the other would do.

The squirrel screeched EEEEEEEEE.

His fur stood out straight,
and his paws left the floor.

The boy squealed, "EWWWWWWW," then
turned on his heels, and flew out the door.

The squirrel dropped his nut on the floor and flew
out the window so high, wondering whatever
was wrong with this frightening guy?

With a start, the boy gasped
and flew across the room to look down at the dirt,
so sure he would find his flying squirrel
on the ground, broken and hurt.

But with legs thrown out and his fur spread wide,
the squirrel, he saw had landed in a tree.
Light as a feather, he swayed in the breeze,
eyes shining bright, happy and free.

The boy smiled, then laughed as they
stared eye to eye, having been to the brink.
Then the squirrel turned and left,
but not before giving the boy a slight wink.

What a story to tell of the night he just had.
What a wonderful tale to relate to his Dad.
How brave he had been;
how clever too! To have found the critter
and seen to his rescue.

The house was now quiet, and life went on
without a sound or a hitch.
No more—

Skitterarich, skit skit,
skitter skit, skitterarich
skitterarich skitterarich itch.

The End

CPSIA information can be obtained
at www.ICGtesting.com
Printed in the USA
LVIC04n0757051215
465138LV00010B/101

9 781681 110301